The Apple Tree's Discovery

To Sonia and Mordechai, who inspire me with their kavannah
and talents: her calligraphy and his hazzanut – P.S.

To my parents who introduced me to stories,
to my children who listened so attentively,
to my grandchildren who started listening when my children
stopped, and to my husband who is so patient. – R.E.D.

To Rabbi Avi Weiss, whose telling of a version of this story in a
Midrash Workshop years ago reached our hearts. We tell this
story with his blessing and permission. – P.S. and R.E.D.

For mom, dad, and brother—thank you for believing in me! – W.W.L.

Titled "The Apple Tree's Discovery," this story, co-authored by Peninnah Schram and
Rachayl Eckstein Davis, has been published in the anthology *Chosen Tales: Stories Told by
Jewish Storytellers*, edited by Peninnah Schram and published by Jason Aronson. Permission
for this publication has been granted by the authors. A version of the story also appeared
in *Apples and Pomegranates* by Rahel Musleah, published by Kar-Ben Publishing in 2004.

KAR-BEN Publishing
A division of Lerner Publishing Group, Inc.
241 First Avenue North
Minneapolis, MN 55401 U.S.A.
800-4KARBEN

Website address: www.karben.com

Library of Congress Cataloging-in-Publication Data

Schram, Peninnah.
    The apple tree's discovery / by Peninnah Schram and Rachayl
Eckstein Davis ; illustrated by Wendy W. Lee.
        p. cm.
    Summary: A little apple tree in the middle of a forest of majestic
oaks longs to have stars in its branches as the tall oak trees seem to
have, but God says that the apple tree should be satisfied with what it
has.
    ISBN 978–0–7613–5130–6 (lib. bdg. : alk. paper)
    [1. Trees—Fiction. 2. Apples—Fiction. 3. Seasons—Fiction. 4. Stars—
Fiction. 5. Self-acceptance—Fiction.] I. Davis, Rachayl Eckstein. II. Lee,
Wendy W., 1985– ill. III. Title.
PZ7.S3774Ap 2012
[E]—dc23   2011022104

Manufactured in the United States of America
1 – DP – 8/4/11

The Apple Tree's Discovery

By Peninnah Schram & Rachayl Eckstein Davis

Illustrated by Wendy W. Lee

KAR-BEN
PUBLISHING

In a great oak forest where the trees grew tall and majestic, there was a little apple tree. It was the only apple tree in that forest, and it stood alone.

Winter came. As the snow fell to the forest floor, it covered the branches of the little apple tree. The forest was quiet and peaceful.

One night the little apple tree looked
up at the sky and saw a wonderful sight.
The stars in the sky appeared to be hanging
on the branches of the oak trees.

"Oh God," whispered the little apple tree,
"how lucky those trees are to have such
beautiful stars hanging on their branches. I
want more than anything in the world to have
stars. Then I would feel truly special."

God looked down on the apple tree and
said gently, "Have patience, little apple tree."

Time passed. The snows melted and spring came to the land. Tiny white and pink buds appeared on the apple tree. Birds came to rest on its branches. People walked by and admired the beautiful blossoms.

All summer long, the apple tree continued
to grow. The branches filled with leaves,
forming a canopy overhead.
   But night after night, the little tree looked
up at the millions upon millions of stars.

"Oh, God," the tree cried, "I want more than *anything* in the world to have stars on my branches and in my leaves, just like the great oak trees."

God looked down and said, "Little apple tree, you already have gifts. Your fragrant blossoms fill the air. Your branches offer a resting place for birds. And your leaves offer shade for weary travelers. Isn't that enough?"

The apple tree sighed and answered, "Dear God, I don't mean to sound ungrateful. I appreciate the pleasure I give to others, but what I want more than anything in the world is to have *stars*. Then I would feel truly special."

God smiled and said, "Be patient, little apple tree."

The seasons changed again. It was fall, and the little tree was filled with many beautiful apples. Walking in the forest, people reached up and picked the tasty fruit.

Still, when night fell on the forest, the apple tree looked through the oak trees at the stars and called out, "Oh God, I want more than *anything* in the world to have stars on my branches. Then I would feel truly special."

God asked, "Isn't it enough that you now have wonderful apples to offer?"

The apple tree shook its branches sadly.

At that moment, God caused a hard wind to blow. The apple tree began to sway even more and suddenly apples fell from the top branch. When they hit the ground, they split open.

"Look," commanded God. "What do you see?"
The little apple tree looked down and saw that
right in the center of each apple was a star.
"Stars. I have stars!" the apple tree rejoiced.

"Yes," God laughed. "You do have stars, and
they've been there all along. You just didn't know it."

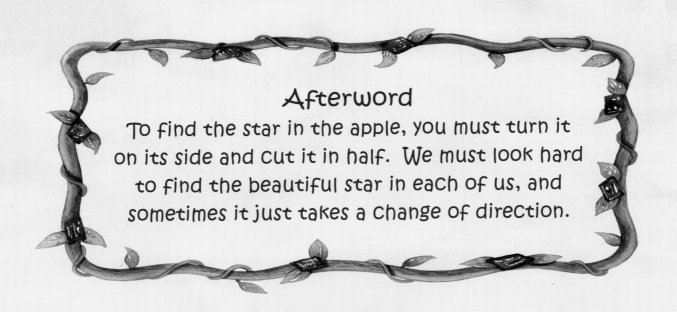

Afterword

To find the star in the apple, you must turn it on its side and cut it in half. We must look hard to find the beautiful star in each of us, and sometimes it just takes a change of direction.

About the Authors and Illustrator

Peninnah Schram is a storyteller, teacher, author, a recording artist, and a Professor at Stern College of Yeshiva University. She is the author of ten books of Jewish folktales, including *Jewish Stories One Generation Tells Another, Stories Within Stories: From the Jewish Oral Tradition,* and *The Hungry Clothes and Other Jewish Folktales.* She has also recorded a CD, *The Minstrel and the Storyteller*, with singer/guitarist Gerard Edery. Ms. Schram has received the Covenant Award for Outstanding Jewish Educator and the National Storytelling Network Lifetime Achievement Award.

Rachayl Eckstein Davis is a freelance storyteller, creative dramatist and educator. She received her B.A. from Stern College and her M.A. from New York University. She has taught pre-school, run a Hebrew Library program, and directed dramatic productions in a Yeshiva high school. This is her first children's book.

Wendy W. Lee is a freelance illustrator based in Queens, New York. She graduated from Fashion Institute of Technology with a B.F.A. in toy design. She creates her whimsical illustrations in watercolor.